VISIT US AT
www.abdopublishing.com

Reinforced library bound edition published in 2010 by Spotlight, a division of the ABDO Group, 8000 West 78th Street, Edina, Minnesota 55439. Spotlight produces high-quality reinforced library bound editions for schools and libraries. Published by agreement with Warner Bros.—A Time Warner Company. All rights reserved. Used under authorization.

Printed in the United States of America, Melrose Park, Illinois.
092009
012010

 PRINTED ON RECYCLED PAPER

Library of Congress Cataloging-in-Publication Data

Strom, Frank.
  Scooby-Doo and The mystery date / writer, Frank Strom ; penciller, Vincent Deporter ; colorist, Paul Becton ; letterer, Tom Orzechowski. -- Reinforced library bound ed.
     p. cm. -- (Scooby-Doo graphic novels)
   ISBN 978-1-59961-689-6
  1. Graphic novels. I. DePorter, Vince. II. Scooby-Doo (Television program) III. Title. IV. Title: Mystery date.
  PZ7.7.S79Sc 2010
  741.5'973--dc22

                              2009032894

All Spotlight books have reinforced library bindings and
are manufactured in the United States of America.

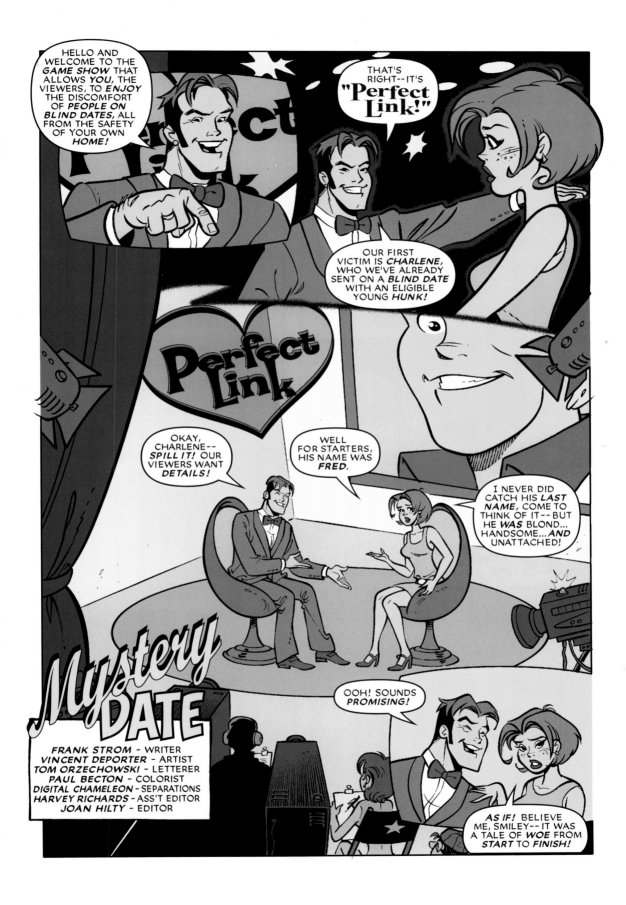

FRANK STROM - WRITER
VINCENT DEPORTER - ARTIST
TOM ORZECHOWSKI - LETTERER
PAUL BECTON - COLORIST
DIGITAL CHAMELEON - SEPARATIONS
HARVEY RICHARDS - ASS'T EDITOR
JOAN HILTY - EDITOR

"WHILE EVERYONE ELSE WAS RUNNING SCARED, *FRED* DIDN'T EVEN BAT AN EYE--

"--IT'S *ALMOST* AS IF HE'D DONE THIS *BEFORE!* NOT TOO *LIKELY*, RIGHT?

"HA! THE NIGHT WAS YOUNG--I HAD *MUCH* TO LEARN!"

SLOOSH

GRROWF?!?

THAT WAS *SUPER*, FRED-- BUT WHO *IS* IT?

ELEMENTARY, CHARLENE! THE ONLY *POSSIBLE* CULPRIT IS...THE CROOKED *RESTAURANT MANAGER!*

GOOD GUESS...BUT IT'S *NOT HER!*

WHAT ARE *YOU* DOING HERE, *VELMA?*

GETTING A *SNACK* AND PROVING YOU *WRONG*, I'M AFRAID. SEE? IT'S REALLY THE DISGRUNTLED *SHORT ORDER COOK!*

DARN! I WAS SO *SURE...!*

SO WHAT HAPPENED *NEXT?*

YOU MEAN *BEFORE* I BARFED...?

WELLL... AT LEAST YOU HAD *DINNER!*

IF THAT'S WHAT YOU WANNA CALL IT. *BARF!*

HE ACTUALLY THREW YOU TO THE *MONSTER?*

IT WASN'T ANYTHING *PERSONAL*, YOU UNDERSTAND-- HE JUST NEEDED A *DECOY!* BRRR!

CERTAINLY WE CAN ALL SEE HOW THAT WOULD *RUIN* A GIRL'S EVENING--

--I MEAN, YOU NEVER GOT TO SEE HOW THE *MOVIE* ENDED!

HA HA HA HA HA

SO...*THEN* WHAT HAPPENED?

AS YOU CAN IMAGINE, MY *FAITH* IN THIS GUY WAS STARTING TO *WAVER*...

"...TO SAY NOTHING ABOUT MY *NERVES!* I WAS A *WRECK!* I WAS *SHAKING* LIKE A LEAF! DEVELOPING A NERVOUS *TWITCH!* COMING *UNGLUED!*

"BUT MR. *ROMEO* HAD THE PERFECT *CURE* FOR WHAT AILED ME--

"--DANCING TILL DAWN!"

WOW! ISN'T THIS *GREAT*, CHARLENE?

T-T-TERRIFIC...

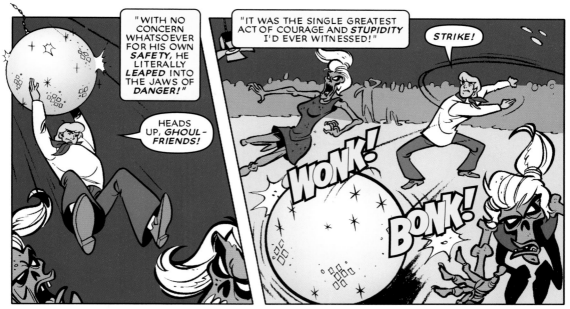

THE END

LIKE, YOU DON'T HAVE TO BE PSYCHIC TO KNOW THAT KOOKY-LOOKING GUY IS *BAD NEWS!*

IT COULDN'T HAVE BEEN SOMEONE OUT OF A *NORMAN ROCKWELL* PAINTING! IT HAD TO BE *THIS* GUY, DIDN'T IT?

I AGREE WITH YOU, SHAGGY. HE SURE IS CREEPY.

WHO IS HE ANYWAY? IT SAYS *"IL DIAVOLO."* DOESN'T THAT MEAN...

IL DIAVOLO

THE DEVIL.

REVIL? ROOOOOOH.

I KNEW IT!

SMACK

IT COMES FROM A FOLK-TALE CALLED *"IL TIGNOSO"*-- *"THE MANGY ONE."* THE STORY IS ABOUT A KING'S SON WHO WEDS A PRINCESS. BUT *BEFORE* THAT...

"...THE YOUNG PRINCE DISCOVERED THAT THE MAN HE BELIEVED TO BE HIS GODFATHER WAS NONE OTHER THAN THE *DEVIL.* HE WAS ONLY ABLE TO ESCAPE HIM THROUGH THE USE OF *THREE* OBJECTS --

"A *COMB,* WHICH BECAME AN *IMPENETRABLE FOREST;*

"A *SIEVE* WHICH TURNED INTO A *MUCK-FILLED MARSH;*

"AND A CAKE OF *SOAP* WHICH TRANSFORMED INTO A *SLIPPERY MOUNTAIN!*"

LAST NIGHT, HE CEASED BEING A STORY, AND CAME TO LIFE--RIDING OUT OF THE PAINTING, AND GALLOPING THROUGH THE HALLS OF THE MUSEUM, AS IF *SEARCHING* FOR SOMETHING!

NOTHING COULD STOP HIM. I *SHUDDER* TO REMEMBER!

WE KNOW WHAT HE'S LOOKING FOR.

IN YOUR COLLECTION, YOU HAVE A STRANGE, UNCUT, LUMINOUS *GREEN STONE*--LIKE THE ONE IN THIS PHOTO.

WHY, YES-- *"THE CASTAFIORE EMERALD"*! THOUGH IT'S NOT ACTUALLY AN EMERALD, BUT IS BELIEVED TO BE AN EVEN RARER, AND UNCLASSIFIED STONE...

MR. CALVINO, CAN YOU SHOW IT TO US RIGHT AWAY? WE'RE SORT OF IN A RACE AGAINST TIME...

HMM. THAT MIGHT BE PROBLEMATIC. I'M NOT EXACTLY CERTAIN WHERE THE STONE *IS*.

YOU SEE, IT WAS REMOVED FROM THE COLLECTION SEVERAL DAYS AGO.

THEN WE'RE TOO LATE!

AGAIN, THE THIEF HAS ELUDED US!

NO, NO. THE CASTAFIORE EMERALD WAS REMOVED FROM THE EXHIBIT FOR *CLEANING* PURPOSES.

RIGHT NOW, IT'S PACKED AWAY IN ONE OF MANY BOXES UNTIL OUR STAFF GETS TO IT.

I DON'T KNOW WHICH BOX, BUT I KNOW WHICH ROOM. COME WITH ME.

TOGETHER, WE SHOULD FIND IT IN NO TIME!

SNORT!

?

!?

Mmmmph!

THIS IS THE ROOM WHERE MUCH OF THE RESTORATION IS DONE ON THE POTTERY, SCULPTURE AND JEWELRY.

THE CASTAFIORE EMERALD COULD BE IN JUST ABOUT *ANY* OF THESE BOXES.

JINKIES, THIS COULD TAKE A WHILE. HAS THE DEVIL BEEN IN THIS ROOM, YET?

NO, HE MAY NOT KNOW THAT IT'S NO LONGER ON DISPLAY...

...WHICH MUST BE WHY HE'S SEARCHING THROUGH ALL THE EXHIBIT HALLS!

THEN THIS MAY GIVE US THE CHANCE WE NEED TO BEAT HIM.

DAPHNE AND I WILL GO SEE IF ANY CLUES CAN BE FOUND LEADING US TO THIS DEVIL. VELMA, YOU AND THE OTHERS LOOK FOR THE CASTAFIORE EMERALD!

ONCE YOU'VE FOUND IT-- HOLD ON TO IT, NO MATTER WHAT!

RESSIR! ROO RAN ROUNT ON RUSS!

HEY FREDDIE, IF YOU PASS A VENDING MACHINE, LIKE, BRING US A *SNACK!* THAT STONE WILL BE EASIER TO HOLD ON TO IF OUR HANDS ARE *STICKY* WITH *ITALIAN CANDY!*

THAT'S FUNNY. THAT *SECURITY GUARD* WHO'D BEEN FOLLOWING US SINCE WE GOT HERE IS NO LONGER AROUND.

WONDER WHERE HE IS?

LET'S ASK THAT *JANITOR* UP AHEAD IF HE'S SEEN ANYTHING. HE'S BOUND TO KNOW THIS BUILDING EVEN BETTER THAN ANY GUARD.

EXCUSE ME, WE WERE WONDERING IF WE MIGHT HAVE A WORD WITH YOU?

?

NO, SORRY. NO SPEAK ENGLISH.

ALLORA PARLI ITALIANO?*

NO, NO.

**你說話
好像
帶中文口音。

我能問你
幾個問題嗎？

* "HOW ABOUT ITALIAN?"

** ‹IS THAT A CHINESE ACCENT?›
‹COULD I ASK YOU A FEW QUESTIONS?›

SORRY, I NO SEE ANYTHING. TODAY, FIRST DAY ON JOB.

BUT, BUT... ⸮SIGH⸮

FREDDIE, DID THAT JANITOR LOOK *FAMIL--*

NEIGHHH! ⸮SNORT⸮

CLOP CLOP CLOP CLOP CLOP CLOP

THAT SOUNDED LIKE A *HORSE!* THOSE HOOF BEATS ARE COMING FROM *BELOW* US!

WAIT HERE--I WANT TO GET A LOOK AT OUR MYSTERIOUS DEVIL!

CLOP CLOP CLOP CLOP CLOP CLOP CLOP

MWAH-HA-HA-HA-HA-HA!

?!!

≶GROAN≷ IT HAD TO BE MY *CANDY BAR* THAT HE GRABBED!

RHE'S RUMMING RACK! RAYBE RHE'LL TRADE!

VELMA, I'M GLAD IT WAS ONLY *YOU* AND NOT THE *DEVIL!*

DID YOU FIND ANY CLUES AS TO WHO HE IS?

NO, BUT I'VE GOT *ONE* SUSPECT...

...AND SOMETHING SIGNOR CALVINO SAID EARLIER GAVE ME AN IDEA ON HOW TO STOP HIM, TOO!

RUN, RAGGY, RUN!

THEN WE'D BETTER HURRY-- IT SOUNDS LIKE SCOOBY AND SHAGGY ARE IN NEED OF A *RESCUE!*

WHOAH-OH-OH-OH!

OOF!

NICE WORK, DAPHNE!

WELL, WE DIDN'T HAVE A *COMB* OR A *SIEVE* LIKE IN THE MYTH--

--BUT THIS IS THE SECOND TIME *"THE SHAGGY ONE"* WAS SAVED FROM THE DEVIL BY A *CAKE OF SOAP!*

BUT WHO IS *THIS?*

I-I DON'T KNOW! I THOUGHT FOR SURE IT WAS YOUR NEW JANITOR!

WHAT? THERE *IS* NO NEW JANITOR. NONE OF OUR JANITORS IS HERE TONIGHT. I THOUGHT IT WOULD BE TOO DANGEROUS!

BUT, FREDDIE AND I BOTH SAW HIM...

WAIT! IT WAS THE SAME MAN I SAW IN PARIS, AND IN RUSSIA WHEN WE CAPTURED THE BABA YAGA! HE MUST BE INVOLVED!

BAD NEWS. THE STONE'S NOT WITH OUR DEVIL HERE.

MY GUESS IS DAPHNE'S MYSTERY MAN HAS IT...

"...AND IS LONG GONE BY NOW."

ONLY *FOUR* STONES LEFT-- BUT THOSE *MEDDLING KIDS* ARE MAKING THINGS MORE DIFFICULT.

I'LL HAVE TO TAKE CARE OF THEM ONCE AND FOR ALL... IN *DAMASCUS!*

TO BE CONTINUED...